FOCUS ON THE FAMILY PRESENTS

Poison at the Pump

BOOK 25

CHRIS BRACK AND SHEILA SEIFERT
ILLUSTRATIONS BY SERGIO CARIELLO

TYNDALE

FOCUS ON THE FAMILY® • ADVENTURES IN ODYSSEY®
TYNDALE HOUSE PUBLISHERS • CAROL STREAM, ILLINOIS

This book is dedicated to

C.B. – Brad, Jordan, Bailey, Clayton, and Jack.

S.S. – Penelope, Rose, Blakely, Zion, and Kolby.

Poison at the Pump
© 2020 Focus on the Family. All rights reserved.

A Focus on the Family book published by Tyndale House Publishers, Carol Stream, Illinois 60188.

The Imagination Station, Adventures in Odyssey, and *Focus on the Family* and their accompanying logos and designs are federally registered trademarks of Focus on the Family, 8605 Explorer Drive, Colorado Springs, CO 80920.

TYNDALE and Tyndale's quill logo are registered trademarks of Tyndale House Publishers.

No part of this publication may be reproduced, stored in a retrieval system, or transmitted in any form or by any means—electronic, mechanical, photocopy, recording, or otherwise—without prior written permission of Focus on the Family.

All Scripture quotations have been taken from *The Holy Bible, English Standard Version.* Copyright © 2001 by Crossway Bibles, a publishing ministry of Good News Publishers. Used by permission. All rights reserved.

With the exception of known historical figures, all characters are the product of the authors' imaginations.

Cover design by Michael Heath | Magnus Creative

For Library of Congress Cataloging-in-Publication Data for this title, visit http://www.loc.gov/help/contact-general.html.

For manufacturing information regarding this product, please call 1-800-323-9400.

For information about special discounts for bulk purchases, please contact Tyndale House Publishers at csresponse@tyndale.com, or call 1-800-323-9400.

Printed in the United States of America

ISBN: 978-1-58997-974-1

26 25 24 23 22 21 20
7   6   5   4   3   2   1

Contents

Cracked

Beth sat on a wooden crate in the basement of Whit's End. The room was filled with gadgets and tools. Someday Mr. Whittaker, also called Whit, would use each of them in one of his inventions.

Beth's cousin Patrick stood next to the newest Imagination Station. Its shiny black hood was open. Patrick wore large magnifying goggles.

Beth laughed. "Your goggles make your eyes look enormous," she said.

Patrick laughed too.

The sharp sound of metal scraping metal filled the air.

Beth put her hands over her ears.

"Sorry about that," Whit said. He was tinkering with the engine of the Imagination Station. His white hair bobbed up and down. "That should do it."

Whit stood and wiped his hands on his white apron.

"What are you fixing?" Beth asked.

"I'm not fixing anything," Whit said. "I'm improving the Imagination Station."

"How?" Patrick asked. "It's already perfect."

"Well, thank you," Whit said. "I added a new gadget. It stops germs from traveling from one adventure to the next. Let's say you catch a cold on your adventure. You won't have it when you return to the Model T."

"Oh good," Beth said. "I hate colds."

Whit tilted his head, as if listening. "Oh no!" he said. "Duck!"

Patrick dove to the ground.

Beth hopped off the crate and shielded her face with her hands.

Ping! Boing! Ping!

Two springs shot out of the engine.

The parts landed on the tile floor near Patrick.

"Anyone hurt?" Whit asked.

"Not me," Patrick said. He picked up the springs.

"I'm fine," Beth said.

Patrick handed the parts to Whit.

"Thanks," Whit said. "Let's see. They should go here and here."

Whit reached into the Model T's engine. He said, "Tesla made the container for the power source out of glass. I used it to rebuild the Imagination Station. I hope the springs didn't smash into it."

Beth walked closer to the Imagination Station. She remembered Tesla from an earlier adventure. He was an inventor like Whit.

"Is it broken, Mr. Whittaker?" Patrick asked.

Whit's hands reached deeper into the engine. "I think it's fine," Whit said.

Beth peered under the Model T's hood. It looked very different from a normal car engine. Rods and hoses went in all directions.

Whit pointed to a glass tube.

"The Imagination Station doesn't run on gas like other cars. It runs on this bubbling liquid," Whit said. "The glass holding the liquid is only half full. The Imagination Station needs time to make more."

"Can we help?" Patrick asked.

"You can," Whit said. "The three liquids inside the glass can be found in different places and times."

Whit's eyes twinkled.

Beth knew what that meant. She said, "We get to go on an adventure!"

Patrick took off his goggles. "I'm ready," he said. He jumped into the driver's seat of the Model T.

Beth climbed into the passenger seat.

Whit closed the Model T's hood. He said, "The Imagination Station will land near the liquid." He picked up a small black box. It had a metal wand at the end of a curly cord. He handed it to Patrick.

"Stick the wand in any liquid," Whit said. "Then look at the button on the box. A green light means you've found the right one."

Patrick nodded. He put the small box in his pocket.

"There's only one liquid at your first stop," Whit said.

"What should we do with it?" Patrick asked. "Once we find it."

"Place it here," Whit said. He showed them a compartment on the passenger side of the car.

"It smells like lemons now," Beth said.

"I smell oranges," Patrick said.

Whit said, "I smell them too." He lay down on the floor. Then he slid under the Imagination Station.

Beth sniffed. She also smelled pears and peaches.

Whit slid out from under the car. He stood up. "The spring must have cracked the power source after all. There's a very slow leak. We're smelling the liquid that is leaking."

"Don't worry," Patrick said. "We'll find the liquid and hurry back. Then you can fix the Imagination Station."

"You can't travel in the Imagination Station now," Whit said. "I need to fix it first." He frowned.

"How will the Imagination Station get the right liquids?" Beth asked.

"I don't know," Whit said. His eyes looked sad.

Beth undid her seat belt. *Our adventures have come to an end,* she thought. Beth felt sad too.

Patrick tried to undo his seat belt. But the latch was stuck. He pulled hard on it. His hand slipped. His elbow hit the red button in the middle of the steering wheel.

"No!" Whit said.

"No!" Beth and Patrick shouted together.

The Imagination Station's hum drowned out their voices.

The lights on the dashboard blinked. The Model T whirled and shook. It moved from side to side. Small droplets of color swirled around them. The smell of fruit was strong.

We'll be stuck in the past forever! Beth thought.

Then everything went black.

Closed

Patrick undid his seat belt and looked toward the passenger seat. Beth wasn't there. The Imagination Station must have sent her to a different location.

Patrick needed to find the first liquid to fix the Imagination Station. He needed to find Beth, too. Traveling together would use less of the Model T's power source. He jumped out of the Imagination Station and slammed the door shut.

He sniffed. The air smelled like a swimming pool next to a garbage dump.

Patrick looked down. White powder covered the brick-lined street.

He looked up. Three-story buildings were across from him. Many of them had shops on the ground floor. A bonnet shop was next to a hardware store. A bakery was beside a shop that sold oil.

We're in a city, Patrick thought.

The Imagination Station faded.

Patrick ignored his fear. The Imagination Station *would* return. He just had to find the right liquid.

A woman came out of a building with the number forty on it. She carried two wooden buckets. Strands of brown hair escaped her white cap. She set down one bucket. She tossed dirty water from the other into the street.

"Hello," Patrick called.

The woman looked over at him. "I usually toss my wash water in the cellar drain," she said. She had an English accent. "But I found myself outside today. So I dumped it here."

The woman sounded troubled.

"I'm looking for a special liquid," Patrick said. Sweat trickled down his back. He felt overdressed in his dark pants, vest, and long-sleeved white shirt. "Do you know of any important liquids nearby?"

The woman pointed to a pump. "We get our water here. I'd help you pump some, but the handle is too heavy," she said.

Patrick looked at her buckets. "Do you need water?" he asked.

The woman nodded.

"My name's Patrick," he said. "I'll pump it for you."

"You're kind," the woman said. "My name's Mrs. Lewis."

Patrick took the wooden bucket from her hand. The bucket smelled like spoiled meat.

Mrs. Lewis picked up the second bucket. It was cleaner.

Mrs. Lewis followed Patrick to the pump. She held her bucket under the spout.

Patrick pushed the handle up. Then he pulled it down. It was heavy. Clean water spurted into the bucket.

Patrick kept pumping until the bucket was full.

A horse-drawn carriage passed them at a brisk clip. Its wooden wheels rattled over the bricks.

Patrick noticed there were no other people on the streets.

"Where is everyone?" Patrick asked.

"Anyone with family outside of London has fled," Mrs. Lewis said. "The air is filled with disease."

Patrick pumped water into the second bucket. "People are afraid of the air?" he asked.

Mrs. Lewis nodded. "They stay inside and close their shutters," she said.

Patrick picked up both buckets. His arms ached from their weight.

"My oldest, my son, used to help fetch our water. He died when he was five," she said. Tears formed in her eyes. "My baby girl died a few days ago."

No wonder Mrs. Lewis is troubled, Patrick thought. *She just lost her baby.*

"I'm sorry she died," Patrick said.

Mrs. Lewis wiped her tears. "She was only six months old," she said.

They walked toward her building.

"This is a big house," Patrick said.

Mrs. Lewis opened the front door. "A rich family once lived here," she said. "But they left years ago. Now twenty poorer families rent these rooms."

Patrick followed her inside.

"My husband, Thomas, and I are very fortunate," Mrs. Lewis said. "Most buildings have five people to a room. We rent the parlor. We've divided it into two rooms." She opened her apartment door.

The room held two chairs, a table, and a shelf. A large fireplace was on one side. A doorway led to a second room.

"Set one bucket by the door," she said. "I'll do the laundry with it."

Patrick put the less clean bucket by the door. His arm felt so much lighter.

Mrs. Lewis pointed to a stool. "The drinking

water goes there," she said. She handed
Patrick a ladle. "Help yourself."

Patrick set the clean water on the stool.
"Thank you," he said. He was thirsty. He
dipped the large spoon into the water and
drank from it. The water was refreshing.

Someone moaned from the next room.

"I'm here, Thomas," Mrs. Lewis called.
She hurried to him.

Patrick hung the curved end of the ladle
on the bucket. Then he peeked into the
second room. A police officer's uniform rested
over an empty wooden crib.

Thomas was lying on a low bed. He was
pale and thin.

"I'll be going now," Patrick said.

"Thank you for your help," Mrs. Lewis said.
She didn't turn around.

Patrick felt bad for Mrs. Lewis. Her baby
had died. Now her husband was sick.

Patrick walked back outside. He took the box with the wand out of his pocket. A small key fell to the ground.

The Imagination Station must have given it to him. He returned the key to his pocket.

Patrick hurried to the pump. He pulled its handle up and down. He stuck the wand into the water. No green light appeared on the box.

A teenager neared the pump. "Hello there," he said. "I'm Clyde."

The teen had dark-brown hair and tan skin. A few freckles dotted his nose. He was dressed like Patrick.

"Hello," Patrick said. "I'm Patrick."

Clyde held the handle of a large wooden box at his side.

An older man with long sideburns walked toward them.

Clyde set down his wooden box with a heavy thud. It was full of tools.

Patrick pulled up the handle on the pump.

"Stop!" the older man shouted. He reached for the handle. His long black jacket flew out behind him.

"Hello, Dr. Snow," the teen said. "Is this it?"

"Yes," Dr. Snow said. He grabbed the pump's handle in mid-air. "You can't get water from here. As of today, September 8, 1854, the Broad Street pump is closed!"

Patrick's eyes widened. He had just had a drink of water from this pump. *Why is this man closing it?* he wondered.

Dr. John Snow

Dr. Snow had on a gray vest beneath his jacket. He wore a bow tie in front of a stiff white collar. "Clyde, you can start work," Dr. Snow said.

He then turned to Patrick. "The pump is closed. Now off you go."

Have I done something wrong? Patrick wondered. He said, "Where am I supposed to go?" He let go of the handle and looked around.

Clyde took a wrench out of his toolbox.

Dr. Snow let go of the handle too. He said, "Where are your parents?"

Patrick hated that question. He said, "My parents aren't here." He didn't want to lie.

"You're an orphan," Dr. Snow said. He waved toward a yellow flag at the end of the street. "There are so many orphans now."

Patrick looked at the yellow flag. "The flag means the neighborhood has orphans?" he asked.

"No," Dr. Snow said. "It warns people to stay away from the infection here."

Dr. Snow pointed across the street to Hiram's Oil Store. A paper was posted in the window. He said, "The Board of Health notice tells about the cholera infection."

Maybe Mr. Lewis was sick with cholera.

"We're safe now," Clyde said. "They put

down the white powder." He placed the wrench head around a bolt on the pump.

Patrick bent down and touched the flour-like substance. Then he brought his finger to his nose.

It smells like a swimming pool, he thought.

"The powder is chloride of lime," Dr. Snow said. "And it doesn't stop cholera!"

"Of course it does," Clyde said. "The smell keeps the infection from getting into the air." Clyde kept working on the pump.

"That's nonsense," Dr. Snow said. "I've been studying this disease for years. I don't know exactly what cholera is. But I've mapped it. I've tracked it to the water from this pump."

Was cholera in the water? Patrick wondered. He felt sick.

A blonde-haired girl without shoes walked toward them. She held a wooden bucket.

"Hi, Rosie," Clyde said.

"Hi, Clyde," she said. She held up her bucket. "Will you pump water for me?"

"No!" Dr. Snow said. "Use a different pump."

"I only need a little," Rosie said.

Dr. Snow shook his head. "This pump is closed," he said.

Rosie glared at Dr. Snow. "You're mean," she said. Then she turned and ran back toward her building.

Clyde took out a hammer. He hit the wrench attached to the pump. The clinking sound echoed down the street.

"Everyone thinks I'm wrong about the cholera outbreak," Dr. Snow said. "But the infection does come from this water."

Thud! The pump handle fell free.

Clyde smiled. "I'll take it to the Board of Guardians," he said.

Dr. Snow tossed Clyde a coin.

The teenager caught it. He dropped it into the toolbox.

"It won't pay the rent. But it's a start," he said. He picked up the pump handle. "Good day."

"'Bye," Patrick said.

Clyde walked away.

"Clyde and Mrs. Lewis think the infection is in the air," Patrick said.

Dr. Snow withdrew a paper from his jacket and unfolded it. The paper looked like a map.

"They're wrong. The water is the problem," Dr. Snow said.

He shook his head. "Hundreds have been infected," he said. "The bars on my map show the deaths from cholera."

Patrick took the map from Dr. Snow. A lot of people around the Broad Street pump had been infected.

"You don't understand. *I* drank water from this pump today," Patrick said. "Do I have cholera?"

"Only time will tell," Dr. Snow said. "Today you were exposed. It could take up to five days to feel the symptoms."

I need to get to a hospital, Patrick thought.

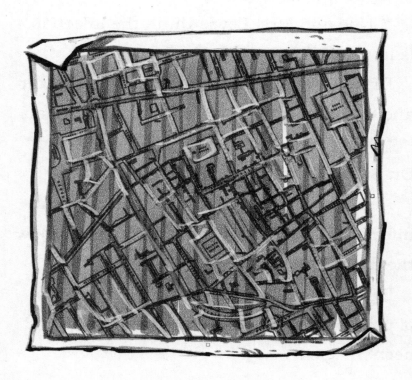

A door from a nearby building opened with a bang.

Patrick looked toward the sound.

Rosie stood by the open door. Two young men and a boy Patrick's age came out. They looked like Rosie. They were probably her brothers. She pointed at Dr. Snow.

Rosie's brothers moved toward them. One had a stick in his hand. The youngest carried Rosie's bucket.

Dr. Snow turned toward them. "What do you want?" he asked.

"Water," one said. He pounded the ground with his stick. "And you're not going to stop us." He raised the stick, as if to hit Dr. Snow.

Dr. Snow turned to Patrick. He shouted, "Run!"

Curate Henry Whitehead

Beth opened her eyes. She was in a kitchen. It had a stone floor and an old-fashioned black stove. Two slices of fresh-baked bread sat on a plate on the counter. Two metal tubs sat on stools.

Beth didn't see Patrick anywhere. She did see a dingy patch on her blue skirt. The skirt ended midway between her knees and feet. A blue shirt was tucked into it.

A black ribbon was in her hand. The numbers 178866 were stitched on it.

Perhaps the Imagination Station had given the ribbon to her. Beth smiled. Maybe the Imagination Station was still working. She tied the ribbon around her ponytail.

A wooden door creaked open. A man walked into the kitchen. He wore black pants and a black shirt. The shirt had black buttons down the front.

"Are you here to wash the breakfast dishes?" he asked.

Beth didn't want to lie. "I know how to wash dishes," she said.

"Fine," he said. "My name is Curate Henry Whitehead. The plates are in the tub with soapy water. There's clean water in the second bucket. What's your name?"

"Beth," she said.

"It's nice to meet you," Henry said. He had dark circles around his eyes. He looked tired. "There's bread and a cup of tea for your payment. Do you have any questions?"

"Yes," Beth said. "What is a curate?"

Henry's eyebrows rose. He looked surprised by the question. "I help the pastor of the church in this London parish," he said. "I'm like a pastor in training."

He gave a merry laugh. "That means I do the jobs no one else wants."

"Like the dishes," Beth said.

Henry laughed again.

"Very similar," he said. "I visit the poor at the workhouse and the sick in the neighborhood. I also preach the service at five in the morning."

"That's early," Beth said. She rolled up her sleeves and turned toward the soapy water. "Are there a lot of sick people to visit?"

Henry sighed. "There are more every day," he said.

"Aren't you afraid of getting sick?" Beth asked.

"My trust is in God alone," Henry said.

A knock sounded at the outside door. Henry hurried to it and pushed it open.

Odd. Most outside doors pull in, Beth thought.

"Hello," a teen boy said. He had dark-brown hair and a few freckles.

"Good morning, Clyde," Henry said. He motioned for Clyde to come into the kitchen.

"I've been meaning to visit your aunt. How is she doing?"

Henry closed the door.

"She has good and bad days," Clyde said. "Have you found my uncle's will?"

"No," Henry said. "But I continue to search for it."

Beth finished washing the dishes. She found a towel to dry them.

"Thank you," Clyde said. "I'm actually here for another reason. Dr. Snow had me take the handle off the Broad Street pump. He thinks cholera is infecting people through the pump's water."

Henry threw up his hands. "Dr. Snow's foolishness is hurting the poor people of my church," he said. "I must convince him to put the handle back on!"

"How will you get him to do that?" Clyde asked.

Henry stopped to think.

"This problem sounds like a mystery," Beth said. "You could ask people. Did they drink water from the pump? Or did they drink water from somewhere else?"

"Excellent idea. I will prove Dr. Snow's theory is wrong," Henry said. "Clyde, would you talk to people on Broad Street? Ask them about their water-drinking habits. I will too."

Henry smiled at Clyde. He said, "You can have a slice of bread before you go. Is that payment enough?"

"Yes!" Clyde said.

Henry nodded. "I'm off," he said. "It was nice meeting you, Beth."

"It was nice meeting you too, Curate Whitehead," Beth said.

Henry shut the door behind him.

Clyde picked up a slice of bread. "You have

the same accent as Dr. Snow's friend," he said. He bit into the bread.

"I don't have an accent," Beth said.

"You're American, aren't you?" Clyde asked. He took another bite. "My uncle's shop has oil from America."

Beth turned to face Clyde. "Is Dr. Snow's friend American?" she asked.

Clyde shrugged. "Maybe," he said. "His name's Patrick."

"That's my cousin," Beth said. "Where did you see him? Can you take me to him?"

Clyde finished his breakfast. "I'd like to," he said. "But I'm working for Curate Whitehead now. I need to deliver water to customers."

"I'll pay for your help," Beth said. "You can have my piece of bread and my cup of tea."

Clyde looked thoughtful. "The streets here are like a maze," he said. "I'll take you to Broad Street." Clyde took a scrap of cloth out of his shirt. He gently folded Beth's slice of bread in it.

"I'll be glad to eat this at dinnertime," he said.

Beth pushed on the back door to open it. The door didn't budge. She pulled. Nothing.

"What's the matter?" Clyde asked.

"The door's locked," Beth said.

Clyde pushed against it. The door wouldn't open for him either.

"It's been barred on the outside," Clyde said.

"Why would anyone bar a door from the outside?" Beth asked.

"The owner of this boardinghouse was married. Her husband grew forgetful," Clyde said. "She changed the way the doors opened. She also put a bar across the outside. That's how he stayed safe inside on her shopping days."

Beth hurried through the dining room to

the front door. She grabbed the handle. The lever went up and down. But the door didn't open.

Clyde followed her into the room. He looked shocked. He said, "Someone doesn't want us to leave. We're trapped!"

Mobbed

Patrick looked over his shoulder. Rosie's brothers were still chasing them. They were upset about the Broad Street pump's handle being removed. They wanted the handle put back on.

Patrick shoved Dr. Snow's map inside his vest. He tried to stay close to Dr. Snow.

Dr. Snow turned right on Portland Street. Patrick followed.

"Give us back our water!" one boy shouted.

Patrick could hear the pounding of their boots on the bricks. They weren't far behind.

A rock flew through the air.

"Ow!" Patrick said. The rock bounced off his shoulder.

"We'll make our own handle!" another shouted.

Patrick's side began to hurt. It felt like someone was pinching him.

Was this the first sign of cholera? he wondered.

Dr. Snow looked behind them.

Patrick looked also.

The young men had stopped running.

Dr. Snow and Patrick slowed to a walk. They turned onto Berwick Street.

"You should be safe now," Dr. Snow said.

Patrick nodded. He still had to catch his

breath. He took out Dr. Snow's map. He
recognized some of the streets now.

"I'm headed to the hospital," Dr. Snow
said. "Are you staying with a relative?"

"No," Patrick said. He folded the map and
handed it back to Dr. Snow. "Can I go with
you to the hospital?"

Dr. Snow frowned as if he didn't want

Patrick to join him. But he said, "Very well. Keep up." He put the map in his jacket pocket. Then he started to walk at a brisk pace.

Patrick had to trot to keep up with Dr. Snow.

Patrick felt relieved. Someone at the hospital would know how to cure him.

"What are the symptoms of cholera?" he asked.

"A twisting pain in your stomach is the first sign," Dr. Snow said. "Eventually you lose all the water in your body. That's what kills you."

Patrick decided he'd only had a side-ache from running.

The buildings were taller and wider than those on Broad Street. They passed a sign that read "Society for the Relief of Widows and Orphans of Medical Men." Other buildings also had signs with official-sounding titles.

They turned down another street and then another.

Patrick saw a large group of people ahead of them.

The group stood next to an iron fence. The iron fence was in front of an enormous white brick building. The building was shaped like a square U.

Patrick pointed. "What's going on there?" he asked.

"It looks like the hospital isn't letting in visitors," Dr. Snow said. "It must be full of cholera patients."

"But I drank water from the pump," Patrick said. "I need to get medicine for cholera."

"Medicine?" Dr. Snow asked.

"Or have a medical test," Patrick said. "Or even get a shot. I need to be cured."

"What do you mean?" Dr. Snow asked. He shook his head. "There's no cure for cholera."

"What?" Patrick asked.

"You need to find a relative or friend," Dr. Snow said. "They can take care of you in case you have the disease." Dr. Snow walked through the group of people toward the gate.

Patrick rushed into the crowd after him.

A man shouted, "You have no right to keep us out!"

Three policemen stood between the mob and the gate. The crowd surged forward. The officers pushed people back.

"I have to know about my aunt!" a woman said. "I told my uncle I'd bring word about Susana."

A woman was crying. A young girl rushed past Patrick and almost knocked him over. A man in rumpled clothes helped Patrick regain his balance.

"Thank you," Patrick said.

"You're not from around here," the man

said. "Your accent is funny. A girl around your age was brought here a couple minutes ago."

A dog barked.

"What was her name?" Patrick asked. "Did they take her inside?"

"They take all the sick inside," the man said.

Oh no, Patrick thought. *Could Beth be sick in this hospital?*

The crowd tightened around Patrick. He felt a sharp elbow to his stomach. Patrick couldn't catch his breath. He felt lightheaded. He fell at Dr. Snow's feet.

Off and Running

Beth went back to the kitchen. There was a large window in the room. But it was made of too many small panes. She couldn't fit through.

"Maybe we can climb out another window," she said. She rushed toward the dining room.

"The dining room window is long and narrow," Clyde called. "It won't work."

Clyde was right. Beth couldn't fit through it either.

"Is there another way out?" Beth asked.

Clyde came into the dining room. "No. There are only two doors," he said.

Beth walked into the front parlor. A sofa was along one wall. A chair with a floral design was in front of the window. Clyde followed her.

"We're not allowed in here," Clyde said. "The boardinghouse owner won't like it."

Beth ignored him. She hurried to the window and tried to open it. The window was painted shut. It wouldn't budge.

"Who would trap us?" Beth asked. She didn't know anyone here. "Do you have enemies?"

Clyde shook his head. "I'm not rich enough to have enemies," he said. "Old Willie doesn't like me. Aunt May is upset with me. But that's all."

Beth frowned.

A staircase was across the room. Beth hurried up the steps.

"You can't go up there," Clyde called.

Beth walked into the first bedroom. The window opened easily. But it was a straight drop to the ground.

"Come back down," Clyde called from the parlor.

Beth hurried across the hallway to another room. It had a large window. She looked outside. There were vines climbing up the side of the house.

Beth knew how to climb a tree. She was sure she could climb vines. She opened the window.

She called to Clyde, "I'll open the back door when I get down."

Beth flung her legs over the window's ledge. Then she turned on her stomach. Her legs dangled outside the window. She reached with her toe to find a foothold.

"What're you doing?" Clyde asked. He stood by the door. "This is someone's bedroom."

"Nice people don't trap other people," Beth said. "I'm not waiting for a bad person to find me." She found a nook for her right foot. She reached for a foothold for her left foot.

"Don't let anyone see you," Clyde said.

Beth found a second foothold. She let go of the sill and grabbed the vines. She slowly started to climb down from the second story. Right foot. Left foot.

Suddenly her left foot slipped. She started to slide.

Beth screamed.

Clyde grabbed for her. Her fingers slipped through his hands.

Beth looked around for help. She saw a tall man and a dainty woman in the distance. The woman wore a black dress and the man had

on a purple jacket. They pointed at her. But they were too far away to help.

Beth tried to scramble back toward the window. She grabbed at vines to keep from falling. Her knuckles scraped the brick wall. Her heart was racing.

The dainty woman and the tall man ran toward her. They were half a block away.

Finally, Beth's left hand grabbed a vine that held.

Beth took a deep breath. She slowly found a nook for her left foot. Then she found one for her right.

"I'm fine," she shouted. She waved to the dainty woman and the tall man.

They didn't wave back.

Beth started climbing down again. Soon she reached the ground. She immediately ran to the kitchen door. She lifted the bar and opened the door.

"Clyde," Beth called.

"I'm here," Clyde said. He stepped outside.

The tall man ran around the corner of the boardinghouse. He had gangly arms and legs. The man reminded Beth of a purple spider. The dainty woman was no longer with him.

"Clyde Wendell," the man shouted. His voice was rough and mean. His purple jacket and pants looked worn.

"Clyde didn't climb out the window," Beth said. "I did. It's my fault."

He was only a few yards away from them. His arms stretched forward. He looked like he wanted to grab them.

Clyde pushed Beth away from the man.

"Don't let Old Willie catch you," Clyde said. "Or you're done for."

They both started running.

They ran through side streets and onto Berwick Street.

"Why is Old Willie chasing us?" Beth asked.

"He's in charge of the workhouse. He wants me to work for him," Clyde said. "But he'd take you, too."

Old Willie kept chasing them.

Berwick Street was filled with people. Large and small carriages were stopped in traffic. Shops and trades-people lined the street. Everyone was yelling.

"Buy my saddles!"

"Beautiful gloves!"

Clyde and Beth dodged through the crowds.

They jumped over the garbage piled next to stalls.

The street smelled like cinnamon, fish, and a horse stable. One man stood in a doorway. He was skinning an eel.

They left Berwick Street. Clyde guided Beth past a row of three-story brick buildings. They were side by side like townhomes. He cut through a narrow lane between two of the buildings.

Beth looked over her shoulder.

Old Willie stopped following them. "I'll get you back!" he shouted. "I'll get you both!" He shook a fist at them.

Escape

Patrick slowly came out of a lovely dream. He had made it back to the Imagination Station. Whit's new device had cleansed him from cholera.

Patrick opened his eyes. It was only a dream.

He was lying on a bed in a long room. Many other beds were in the room. All their

headboards were against the wall. Some of
the patients were moaning. The whole place
smelled like soap.

But now Patrick knew what to do. He had
to find the right liquid. Then the Imagination
Station would return. And
it would cure him.

"Not here, gentlemen,"
a woman said. She had
dark-brown hair and wore
a white-lace cap. A long
white apron covered most
of her black gown.

Dr. Snow stood by the
bed. A man leaned toward
him. "You removed the
pump handle. The poor
in my church now have
to walk many blocks for
water."

"I've saved their lives, Curate Whitehead," Dr. Snow said. "The cholera infection comes through the water at the Broad Street pump."

"How can you say that?" the curate said.

"Look at this," Dr. Snow said. He unfolded a paper. It was the map Patrick had seen before.

"These show the deaths by cholera. Talk to the people in your church. Talk to the sick and to those who aren't sick. Then tell me I'm wrong," Dr. Snow said.

"Enough!" the nurse said.

"I thought you were on my side," the curate said.

"I am," she said. "But first I'm on the side of my patients. This is a sick room. Take your argument outside!"

Both men looked ashamed.

"I'm sorry, Nurse Nightingale," the curate said.

"Forgive me," Dr. Snow said.

Nurse Nightingale pointed toward the door. Both men walked toward it. She looked down at Patrick.

"You're awake. How do you feel?" she asked. "Dr. Snow thought you'd had the wind knocked out of you."

"I can breathe now," Patrick said. "But that may not be enough. I drank water from the Broad Street pump." He waited for Nurse Nightingale to react. But she didn't.

Patrick said, "People drink that water. Then they get cholera."

Nurse Nightingale laughed. "You've been listening to Dr. Snow. I wouldn't be too worried," she said. "Everyone else believes cholera travels through the air."

"The air?" Patrick said. "But then everyone would be sick."

"Is the air dirty in your neighborhood?" Nurse Nightingale asked. "Hundreds of people have breathed the filthy air near Broad Street. That's why they're sick now."

Patrick sat up. He felt better already. The air, not the water, carried cholera. Maybe he had more time to find the right liquid. He didn't need the Imagination Station's cure after all.

Nurse Nightingale gave him a slow smile. "Have you recovered?"

"I have," Patrick said. He stood. "Thank you."

She gave him a nod and turned to help another patient.

Patrick walked out of the room and into a wide hallway. There were no beds there, only white tiles and walls. Patrick saw stairs leading to the second floor, and a door. He didn't see Dr. Snow or Curate Whitehead.

Patrick did see a container of clear liquid. The container sat on a small table in the

corner. The liquid smelled like something
painters used to clean their brushes.

Patrick quickly took the black box out of his
pocket. He stuck the wand in the liquid. The
button didn't turn green. He cleaned the wand
and put it back in his pocket.

Then he remembered Beth. She might be
sick in this hospital. She would need a cure.
She would need the Imagination Station.

He went to the door across the hall. It was
locked.

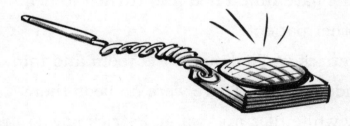

Patrick removed the key from his pocket. He
slid it into the door's keyhole. But his key was
too small. He put it back in his pocket.

Patrick went back into the room with

patients. He wanted to ask Nurse Nightingale about Beth. But she was no longer there. Patrick walked down the aisle. He didn't see Beth in any of the beds.

Another hallway was at the end of the room. It led to another staircase.

"Children aren't allowed in the hospital without parents," a large man said. He had a brown beard. He looked like a hospital guard. The guard walked toward Patrick.

But Patrick couldn't leave without Beth. He hurried to the stairs and climbed them two at a time.

Two closed doors were at the top of the stairs. He opened one. It was a closet.

Patrick heard the clicks of the guard's shoes on the stairs. He ducked beneath the closet's bottom shelf. He rolled into the back corner. Then he grabbed the lower edge of the door and closed it.

Footsteps raced past the closet door. The other door opened and then shut with a bang.

Patrick listened. He was hot and cramped. But he didn't move.

Suddenly, the closet door opened. A draft of air tickled Patrick's face. A woman's button-up boots stood in front of him.

It was Nurse Nightingale. She took linens off a shelf. "It's so hard to keep everything clean," she said to herself. She looked down. "What're you doing here?" she asked.

Patrick rolled out of the closet and stood up.

"I'm looking for my cousin Beth," Patrick said. "Have you seen her? She has dark hair and is around my age."

The other door opened. The guard came barreling through.

Patrick turned toward the stairs.

But the guard grabbed him. "Got you,"

he said. His heavy hand clamped down on Patrick's shoulder.

"What are you doing?" Nurse Nightingale said.

"He's just another orphan who wants to steal food from this hospital. But I've caught you now," the guard said. He pushed Patrick toward the stairs.

"He had the wind knocked out of him. He was a patient," Nurse Nightingale said. "Your cousin's name is Beth, not Elizabeth?"

"Just Beth," Patrick said.

"I have seen so many children," Nurse Nightingale said. "Your cousin's name would have stuck in my mind. She isn't here."

Patrick felt relieved.

The guard pushed him onto the first step.

"Where are you taking this child?" Nurse Nightingale asked. Her voice was stern.

"I am escorting him out of the hospital,"

the guard said. "I don't want him catching cholera."

"Good," she said. "Goodbye, and I hope you find your cousin."

Patrick waved goodbye.

The guard kept pushing. They reached the bottom step.

"You fooled Nurse Nightingale," the guard said. "But you don't fool me. There's a place for thieves like you. And I'm going to take you there."

Pumps & Cisterns

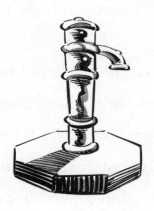

Clyde stopped running and laughed. "I knew he wouldn't follow us this way. We're at the back side of the Broad Street houses," he said. "A lot of people have come down with cholera here."

Beth stopped also. Sweat trickled down her back.

The ground was a mixture of bricks,

stones, and black mud. A small shack was to one side. There was a brick-lined hole in the middle. It was full of water.

"What is that smell?" Beth asked.

"The privies," Clyde said. He pointed to the shack.

Beth had heard of these old-fashioned bathrooms. They didn't have running water. They were like campground toilets, holes in the ground with seats over them.

"I have to get people's water buckets," Clyde said. "Then I'll take you back to Broad Street. I met Patrick at the pump there. Old Willie should be gone by then."

"Okay," Beth said.

Clyde walked toward the back door of one building. Delicate flowers were carved into the gray bricks above the door.

Beth followed him into the building.

The hallway was dingy and dirty. The wooden floor creaked.

Beth followed Clyde up the stairs to the third floor.

Clyde knocked on a door, and then he went in.

Beth looked around the room. There was no kitchen or bathroom. It was only a room with a fireplace, beds, and chairs.

"The bucket's right here, Clyde," an older lady said. She sat in a rocking chair.

The bucket of water must be for cooking, drinking, and washing, Beth thought.

"I wondered if you'd be coming today. It's my birthday," she said. "Who's your friend?"

"This is Beth," he said.

"It's nice to meet you, Beth," the older woman said. "I like your hair ribbon."

"Thank you," Beth said. She untied the ribbon from her hair. Then she held it out to the woman. "Happy birthday!"

"I couldn't," the woman said. But her hand reached for it. "It's real pretty," she said.

She pointed to the numbers 178866. "I was born in 1788. Today I'm 66."

Clyde looked at Beth in surprise and then back to the woman.

Beth smiled. The Imagination Station always knew just what to give her and Patrick. She would remember those numbers, 178866.

Clyde picked up the woman's wooden bucket. "Who brought you water before me?"

"I got it from the cistern in back," the woman said.

Beth wondered what a cistern was. She decided to ask Clyde later.

Another woman was in the opposite corner

of the room. She was talking softly to a small child on a cot. He moaned.

"Is Timothy feeling better?" Clyde asked. He walked over to the other woman.

"I believe he is," the woman said. Her clothes were dull gray.

A toddler sat at her feet. The girl's dirty fingers played with the hem of her mother's skirt.

Clyde asked, "Where's your bucket?"

"I haven't a half penny to give you this week, Clyde," the woman said.

Beth picked up the bucket in the corner by its wooden handle. "I'll fill it for you," she said.

The woman smiled. She turned back to the cot.

"Where did you get your water before me?" Clyde asked.

"Timothy got our water from the Broad Street pump," she said.

Beth had never seen so many people living in such a small room. It was the size of her bedroom.

They left the room and made their way back outside.

Someone tossed dirty water from a bucket through a window. Beth jumped out of its way.

"What did she do that for?" Beth asked.

Clyde laughed. "She wasn't being mean," he said. "Don't people toss water out of the windows in your town?"

"No!" Beth said.

"Here, no one walks directly beneath windows," he said.

"I won't do that again," Beth said. She remembered her question from earlier. "What's a cistern?"

Clyde pointed to the brick-lined hole close to the privy shack. Beth looked at the water. There were tree leaves, dirt, and bugs in it.

"We're not giving your customers that water, are we?" Beth asked.

"No. The cistern holds rainwater," Clyde said.

"The people pay me for pumped water. But a lot of older people drink this water. It's not bad. And it's easier for them to get. Pumping water is hard work," he said.

Beth looked around. "Where's the pump?" she asked.

Clyde said, "Broad Street was the closest pump. Now it's closed. We have to walk to the next pump."

For water? Beth thought. *No wonder Curate Whitehead was upset the Broad Street pump was closed.*

They walked back down the narrow lane between brick buildings. They came out not far from building forty.

Clyde pointed. "That's the Broad Street pump," he said.

The bricks on the street and sidewalk were covered in white powder. The street was almost deserted. Only a blonde-haired girl was outside. She held a bucket and was looking up the spout of the pump.

Beth went over to her. There were many footprints in the white powder by the pump.

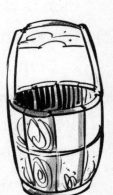

"Hi," Beth said. "Have you seen a boy about my age here?"

The girl nodded.

"Which way did he go, Rosie?" Clyde asked.

Rosie pointed north. "He was with Dr. Snow. My brothers chased them after you broke our pump," she said.

Beth hoped Patrick was okay.

"You usually get your water here, don't you?" Clyde asked.

Rosie nodded. "But only my dad drinks it. My oldest brother brings water home for us. It's from a pump by his work," she said.

"Anyone sick in your family?" Clyde asked.

Rosie frowned. "My dad," she said. "He moans day and night." She kicked a rock on the ground with her bare foot.

Beth hugged Rosie. "I'm so sorry."

"Me too," Clyde said. He started walking away from the pump.

Beth followed him. She would get water for Timothy's mother. Then she'd return and look for Patrick.

Locked Away

The guard took Patrick out of the hospital. They went down many streets to a large, red-brick mansion. Patrick tried to escape. But the guard was too strong.

Patrick counted twenty windows on the front of the two-story building. The flat roof had a white railing around it.

Maybe I can escape from here, Patrick thought.

The guard knocked on a wooden door.

A tall man with thin, gangly arms and legs opened it. "What do you want?" he asked. His gray vest didn't match his purple jacket and pants. His lips held a sour frown.

"Got you another worker, Old Willie," the guard said.

Old Willie looked at Patrick. "He's on the small side," he said. He looked around nervously. "Come in before you're seen."

The guard pushed Patrick through the doorway and into a courtyard. The brick buildings formed a square around it.

The courtyard was filled with people in ragged clothes. They didn't look happy.

"I've got to get back to work," the guard said. He held out his hand.

Old Willie tossed him a coin. "Don't want your hospital cholera here. Get out."

The guard caught the coin and smiled. Then he went back through the door.

Patrick tried to grab the doorknob before it closed. But he wasn't quick enough.

Patrick remembered the key from the Imagination Station. He took it out of his pocket.

He jammed the key into the door's keyhole. It went in easily. But it didn't unlock the door. The key was too small. He stuffed it back in his pocket.

Old Willie held up a large

key. "It only opens with this one," he said. "You belong to me now."

"I don't belong to anyone," Patrick said. "And I won't work for you."

"You'll work, or you won't eat," Old Willie said. "And if you speak back to me again, you'll regret it." He made a fist.

Old Willie scared Patrick. He hoped the Imagination Station would come back for him. He didn't want to live here his whole life.

I have to find the right liquid, he thought.

Old Willie said, "You get porridge for breakfast. Dinner is boiled meat. Supper is bread and tea. We don't sleep more than three to a bed."

The people in the courtyard looked hot and tired. Most were older and moved slowly.

Old Willie said, "We turn flax plants into linen thread. You work and you get to eat."

Patrick watched the people work.

Some crushed a hay-like plant between pieces of wood. Others put the smashed plants on a wall and beat them with paddles. A third group ran the plant through metal combs. The plant changed from being stiff to being soft like hair.

Old Willie pointed to the pile of hay-like plants. "Take the flax to the flax breaks." He pointed to the wooden pieces crushing the plant.

Patrick walked over to the large pile of flax. He sighed.

"Come here, child," an older woman said. She walked toward him. "I'll show you to your room. You can put your things away. Then you can work."

The woman had long gray hair. Her front teeth were missing, and her skin was wrinkled. But her voice was kind.

Patrick didn't have anything. But he followed

her across the courtyard. They went into the building in back of the workhouse.

"It's not so bad here," she said. "You'll get used to it." She went up the stairs slowly.

"I don't want to get used to it," Patrick said.

"No one does at first," she said. She stopped and looked at him. "You need money to pay your way out. Do you have any?" Her eyes gleamed.

She leaned forward. Her hands moved toward him. They looked ready to grab his money.

Patrick shook his head. "I don't have anything," he said.

Her hands dropped to her sides. She looked upset. "That's too bad," she said.

She pointed to the first door in the hallway. "You'll share with Teddy and Liam," she said. "You better get back to work." Her voice was no longer kind. The woman left.

Patrick went into the room.

The room smelled like sweaty socks. There was dirt on the floor. Cobwebs hung in one corner. A small bed rested against a wall. A window was above the bed.

This is a prison for the poor, Patrick thought.

He touched the mattress. It crackled. He bent down. The mattress was stuffed with flax or hay or another plant. It looked too small to hold three people.

Patrick climbed on it and looked out the narrow window. He couldn't escape through it. This day had gone from bad to worse.

People passed by the building. No one looked up.

Patrick took a double look.

This can't be, he thought. Patrick rubbed his eyes.

Aunt May

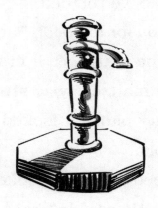

Clyde turned to Beth. "The closest working pump is that way," he said. Clyde pointed down a street. "But I need to check on someone first. It won't take long."

"That's fine," Beth said.

They walked to a narrow alley. It was between Hiram's Oil Store and building number forty.

"She lives in an apartment above the store," Clyde said. "Set your bucket on the ground. We'll take the outside stairs to the second floor." He put his bucket at the bottom of the stairs.

They took the stairs to the second floor. Clyde didn't knock. He just walked in.

The room was much bigger than the other apartment they'd been in. Everything was covered in dust. There was a door at the end of the room.

An old bulldog stood and wagged its tail.

A rope connected the dog to a chair.

"Oscar!" Clyde said. He knelt down. The dog licked his face. "Where's your throne, buddy?"

Beth untied the rope

around Oscar's neck. "You poor thing," she said. She scratched Oscar behind the ears.

Oscar licked her hand.

Clyde took the bread out of his shirt. He gave it to the dog. Oscar ate it in one gulp.

"What will you eat for dinner?" Beth asked.

"A little hunger never hurt anybody," Clyde said.

"How're you doing, boy?" Clyde petted the dog's head.

A woman hurried into the room. Her brown hair was pulled back beneath a white cap. She wore a floor-length black dress.

Beth gasped. This was the dainty woman she'd seen earlier near the boardinghouse. The woman had been with Old Willie.

"Get out," the woman said. "And take that dog with you."

"Aunt May—," Clyde said. He wiped his nose on his sleeve.

"Don't you call me that," May said. "Don't call me anything. I can't help you here."

Clyde sat back. "I came to fill your water bucket," he said. He looked sad.

May said, "I put the bar across the boarding-house door. You needed to stay put. Old Willie should have caught you this morning. Then you'd have a place to sleep."

Beth couldn't believe Clyde's aunt had trapped them in the boardinghouse. She had wanted Old Willie to take Clyde to the workhouse.

"My husband hid his cash and his will," May said. "But he never told me where. Rent's due on this lodging and the shop tomorrow. We can't pay it."

Clyde stood and picked up her empty bucket.

"You can't work or sleep at the oil store

anymore," May said. "It's closed. I can't take care of you. I'm ruined!"

Clyde looked at the floor. "I'll be back with your water soon," he said. A tear escaped his eye and rolled down his check.

Beth followed Clyde to the door. Oscar waddled after them.

"I won't drink it," May said, "unless it's Carnaby water."

Clyde nodded. "I'll get your water at the Carnaby pump, like always," Clyde said.

Beth shut the door behind them.

Oscar hurried down the steps with them. They picked up their buckets and left.

Beth didn't know what to say. She looked back at the store. It had a green door. "Is this your family's store?" she asked.

"Yes, that's it," he said. "Hiram's Oil Store. It's named after my uncle."

"Why do people need oil?" Beth asked. "For cooking?"

"No, the oil we sell is for lamps," Clyde said. "Oil lamps are more modern than candles. There are many different kinds of oils for lamps."

They walked down the street. Beth knew Clyde felt sad. She didn't know how to help him.

Beth asked, "What will your aunt do?"

"I don't know. I'm all she has," Clyde said. "She lost three daughters last week. Then my uncle died from cholera too."

They turned north on Marshall Street.

Clyde blinked quickly as if holding back tears. He picked up his pace and cleared his throat.

Clyde said, "My uncle got me out of the workhouse. He taught me how to run his oil store."

"He sounds like a nice man," Beth said.

"Yes," Clyde said. He looked down at Oscar trotting beside them.

"My uncle loved Oscar. He even let Oscar sleep on an old blanket at the store. He called it his throne," Clyde said. "He was always saying things like that."

Beth shifted her wooden bucket to her other hand. "Why have you been doing odd jobs?" she asked. "Your Aunt May said you worked at the oil store."

"I have the key to the store. But my aunt was right. I can't run the store without my uncle's will or accounts. Now we owe rent on the building," Clyde said. "Curate Whitehead is trying to find the will."

Beth couldn't help Clyde. But maybe he could help her.

"My cousin and I are looking for a liquid. It's for a special invention," Beth said.

"The shop is full of liquids. We have oils from all over the world," Clyde said. "I told you about the one from America. My uncle liked finding unique oils. He wanted to light up the whole country with oil lamps."

Oscar's short legs kept up with them. They turned west down a lane. Then they went north again on Carnaby Street. Soon they reached the pump. There were three people in front of them.

Beth supposed the pump was busier because the Broad Street pump was closed.

Water sloshed onto the ground as people moved their buckets.

Oscar lapped the spilled water on the ground. Then he stood by Clyde and waited.

Soon it was their turn. Clyde quickly filled their three buckets.

"Your bucket is half full," he said. "It'll be easier for you to carry. Besides, only paying customers get full buckets."

They left the pump. Clyde carried his buckets easily.

Beth's half-filled bucket was heavy. Her arm felt stretched.

The two of them made their way back to Marshall Street.

Beth saw the curate in the distance. He was walking toward them.

"He's probably going to the workhouse," Clyde said. He nodded toward a large building behind them. "He goes once a week. He tries to find ways to help those inside. He helped my uncle find me."

The workhouse's brick walls, even the back side, looked like a prison.

"Beth! *Beth!*"

Beth looked around. That was Patrick's
voice. Where was he?

Clyde set down his buckets. He pointed to
a second-story window at the workhouse.

An arm was sticking out of the narrow
opening. It was waving to them.

Oh no, Beth thought. *Old Willie has caught
Patrick!*

11

The Workhouse

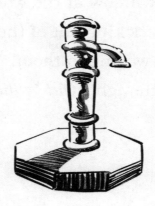

Beth, Clyde, and a bulldog hurried to the workhouse. They stood under Patrick's window.

Beth called up to him, "Patrick, I'm so glad to see you." She put down her bucket. "What're you doing in there?"

"A hospital guard brought me here," he said:

"Old Willie gave him money. I'm a prisoner. You have to get me out of here!"

Clyde set down his buckets. "Old Willie took me the day my dad died. He wants orphans and poor people to work for him," Clyde said.

A man wearing black clothes stopped next to Beth and Clyde. "Hello again," he said to Beth. "Hello, Clyde."

"We're glad to see you. Patrick, this is Curate Henry Whitehead," Clyde said.

Patrick looked at the man. He recognized him. He had argued with Dr. Snow in the hospital.

"This is my cousin Patrick," Beth said.

"Hello, Patrick," Henry said.

"It's nice to meet you, Curate Whitehead," Patrick said.

Henry unfolded a map. "No one in the workhouse has died of cholera," he said. "Maybe we should all stay with you in the workhouse."

Beth and Clyde said, "No!"

Henry laughed.

"I've seen that map before," Patrick said. "That's Dr. Snow's map."

"You're right. I talked to Dr. Snow. He's letting me use it," Henry said.

Henry pointed to the map. "The squares show where people have died from cholera," he said.

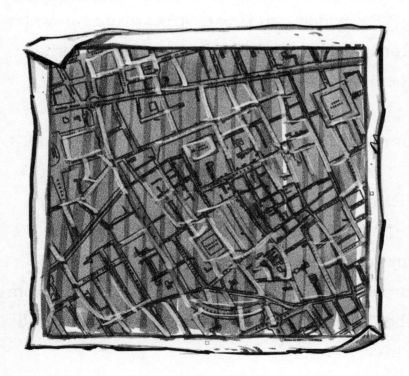

"There are no squares in the workhouse. No one at the workhouse is even sick. I wanted to see this for myself."

"A lot of older widows on Broad Street aren't sick either," Clyde said.

"I noticed them at church last Sunday," Henry said. "Many people didn't attend. But a lot of older women were there."

"The widows on Broad Street drink rainwater from the cisterns," Clyde said. "Unless I bring them pump water."

Patrick thought about Mrs. Lewis. "The pump handle is too heavy for them," he said.

"Where does the workhouse get its water?" Henry asked.

"It has its own pump," Clyde said. "Also, my uncle and cousins drank water from the Broad Street pump. My aunt and I drank from the Carnaby pump. We are the only ones still alive."

Patrick sighed. That wasn't good news for him. He hoped the water from the Broad Street pump didn't carry the infection.

"So, here's what we know," Henry said. "People drank from the cisterns and the Carnaby pump. But they didn't get sick. People drank from the Broad Street pump and did get sick."

Henry scratched his head. "This is all very puzzling. I have a lot of work to do. I need to find the index case," he said.

Patrick leaned closer to the window. He said, "What's an index case?"

"It's the first person to die," Henry said. "It will tell us more about this disease. And the well water needs to be retested."

"Mr. York can do that," Clyde said. "He's a local man."

Beth asked, "What are you testing for?"

Henry folded Dr. Snow's map. "I don't

know. Maybe something was added to the water at Broad Street," he said. "That may be the connection between the water and this illness."

"We need to deliver our water buckets," Clyde said. "But then I can help."

"Me too," Beth said.

"Good," Henry said. "Meet me at the Broad Street pump. I'll get York. He'll need workers to dig down to the pump's water."

"What about Patrick?" Beth asked. "We can't leave him here."

Henry looked up at Patrick. He scratched his head and thought for a moment. Then he said, "Patrick will meet you there also."

Patrick wondered how he'd escape. But he put on a brave face and waved goodbye to Beth.

She waved back. "See you soon," she said.

The bulldog followed Beth and Clyde.

"Were you assigned a job?" Henry asked.

"Yes," Patrick said.

"Go do it," Henry said. "I often visit the poor in the workhouse. But today I have another motive. I want to see for myself that no one here has cholera. Do your job, and act like we've never met."

"Okay," Patrick said. He hoped he could trust Curate Whitehead.

Patrick returned to the courtyard. He went straight to the large pile of flax. He picked up a bundle and set it beside the first flax break. An older man nodded his thanks. Then the man slammed the arm of the flax break down on the flax.

Patrick went back for another bundle. He saw Old Willie open the front door.

Curate Whitehead entered. He spoke to Old Willie. Then he went to people working in the courtyard.

Patrick set a bundle by the second flax break.

Henry talked to the people combing the flax. Then he talked to those beating the plant. Finally he reached those on the flax breaks. He spoke to each person and prayed for some.

Patrick continued carrying the bundles of flax. Sweat trickled down his back.

"Hello, my name is Curate Henry Whitehead. You must be new here," Henry said to Patrick.

Patrick looked down. "I am," he said.

Henry turned from Patrick and went back to Old Willie.

Patrick kept carrying flax bundles.

Dear God, please help the curate get me out of here, he prayed.

Henry held out two coins. Old Willie tried to grab them. But Henry pulled them back. Then Old Willie pointed to Patrick.

Patrick carried an extra-large bundle. He pretended not to notice.

Finally Old Willie walked over to Patrick. "You're going to work for Curate Whitehead today," Old Willie said. "You'd better work hard. Or you'll get the back of my hand. Understand?"

Patrick dropped the flax bundle in his arms. "Yes," he said. He tried to look upset. He walked toward the entrance.

Henry held out the same two coins.

This time, Old Willie greedily grabbed the money. "When will you return the boy?" he asked.

"He'll be digging all day," Henry said. "You can fetch him at dusk."

Patrick walked out of the workhouse with Henry. He didn't care who came to fetch him. Patrick was never going back.

Digging

Clyde and Beth delivered water to Aunt May and the woman with the sick child. Then they gave water to the older woman. She already had Beth's ribbon in her hair.

"Happy birthday again," Beth said.

The woman smiled and showed her the ribbon.

Beth smiled back.

Beth would never forget the numbers

on that ribbon, 178866. She was glad the numbers had made the woman so happy.

Clyde and Beth left and walked down Broad Street. Oscar ran by Clyde's side.

Beth could see the pump and building number forty in the distance. But she didn't see Patrick.

Henry stopped outside the workhouse entrance and turned to Patrick. "I have to go this way to find York," he said.

He pointed. "You need to go that way to reach Broad Street. Your friends will be there. Run!"

Why do I need to run? Patrick wondered. But he did what the curate said. He ran. Soon he wasn't alone. He heard a mean voice behind him.

"Get back here," Old Willie shouted. He

was running after Patrick, and he wasn't far behind. "I changed my mind. Get back to the workhouse."

Patrick ran faster. He turned onto Broad Street.

Clyde, Beth, and the bulldog were already there.

"Old Willie is trying to cheat Curate Whitehead," Patrick shouted. "He wants to take me back to the workhouse."

Clyde and Beth started to run with Patrick. The bulldog followed them.

They all ran away from Old Willie together.

"Come back," Old Willie shouted.

They passed the Broad Street pump. Then they ran up and down the streets.

Old Willie's long legs were gaining on them. "Got you," Old Willie said.

"Help!" Beth shouted.

Old Willie had caught his cousin. Patrick stopped. He turned to face Old Willie. The Imagination Station might never come back for them. But he wouldn't keep running from Old Willie.

Clyde stopped also. He faced Old Willie too.

Old Willie had Beth by the shoulder.

The bulldog growled and slunk toward Old Willie. Its head was low. Its teeth were bared.

"Call off your dog," Old Willie said. He held Beth in front of him.

Beth said, "You're a bully." She struggled to get out of his grasp.

That gave Patrick an idea. "Bullies pick on one person at a time," he said. "I don't think you'll fight all three of us."

Patrick and Clyde took a step forward.

Old Willie took a step back.

The dog kept moving toward Old Willie.

Old Willie let go of Beth. "I'll be back for you," Old Willie said.

He pointed at Patrick. "You're still mine. Curate Whitehead is an honest man. He'll hand you over at the end of the day," he said.

"I'll be waiting for you," Patrick said.

"So will I," Beth said.

Clyde cracked his knuckles.

The dog leaped forward.

"Yeow!" Old Willie shouted. He quickly ran away.

The dog chased him down the street and around the corner.

"Go, Oscar!" Clyde shouted.

Patrick put his arms in the air. "We did it," he said.

Clyde shook his head. "I wish it were true. But he'll be back," he said. "Next time Old Willie will bring more men."

Patrick kicked a loose stone in the street. There had to be a way to get away from Old Willie for good.

They walked back to the Broad Street pump in silence.

A slim man in work clothes was already there. He had sharp blue eyes and held shovels, ropes, and buckets. Rosie's three brothers were beside him.

Patrick supposed they needed the pay. They may not be friends. But they would all work together.

"Hello, Mr. York," Clyde said.

"It's good to see you, Clyde," York said. "And who are you?"

"I'm Patrick. This is my cousin Beth," Patrick said.

"It's nice to meet you," York said. He pointed to Rosie's brothers. "You'll all be digging together."

Clyde nodded a greeting to the other boys.

They nodded back.

Oscar gave a happy bark.

"This is Oscar," Clyde said. He scratched the dog's head. "Where do you want us to dig?"

"Let me think," York

said. He walked around the Broad Street pump. Oscar followed at his heels, his tail wagging.

Patrick pointed to the space between the pump and building forty. "We shouldn't dig on that side," he said. "Mrs. Lewis dumped her dirty water there. She didn't go to the drain in the basement."

"The drain in the basement?" York asked.

Clyde said, "That drain is an old cesspool."

"All cesspools were closed years ago," York said.

"Not this one," Patrick said. "Mrs. Lewis still uses it."

"What's a cesspool?" Beth asked.

"It's a large brick box under the ground," York said. "It holds human waste and dirty wash water."

"Yuck," Beth said.

Digging

York hurried to building forty. He took long strides forward.

"The outside wall of the cesspool should be buried here," he said.

Clyde stood in that spot.

York hurried to the pump. He took long steps toward Clyde. He said, "The wall of the well should be buried here."

Beth hurried to that spot.

Only a few feet were between Clyde and Beth.

Rosie's brothers picked up shovels.

"Do we dig between the two underground brick walls?" Patrick asked.

York nodded. He looked grim.

York suspects something, Patrick thought. He stuck a shovel in the ground. He had no idea what they were about to uncover.

The Problem

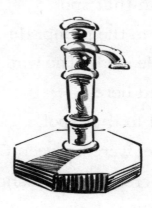

York set up two teams for digging. Clyde,
Patrick, and Beth were one. Rosie's brothers
were the other. One team dug while the
other removed the buckets of dirt. Then they
switched.

The teams worked together for hours. The
trench between the pump and the cesspool
grew deep.

Henry and Dr. Snow arrived and were talking together.

Oscar barked at the edge of the hole.

Beth shoveled dirt into her bucket. So did Clyde. But Patrick filled his bucket with dirt first. Then he handed it to one of Rosie's brothers.

They gave Patrick back the empty bucket and took Clyde's full bucket.

Beth stuck her shovel into the dirt again. She hit something hard. It was the brick wall of the cesspool. Water trickled from it. A bad smell escaped with the water.

"Mr. York," Patrick called. "Beth's found a leak."

York bent over the hole. Then he hurried down into the trench.

"Clear this away," he said. He pointed to dirt along the cesspool bricks.

Clyde dug around them.

York easily pulled a brick out of its place. "That's not good. This wall is falling apart," he said.

Clyde dug next to the Broad Street well's brick wall. Some of the bricks had cracks in them.

Beth stuck her shovel into the ground. "Yuck," she said. "The ground below here is wet."

York examined the ground. "Water from the cesspool is leaking. Everyone out."

The children handed their shovels to Rosie's brothers. They quickly climbed out of the trench.

Clyde said, "Curate Whitehead and Dr. Snow, we found something."

York called up, "Dirty water from the cesspool has leaked into the clean well water." He climbed out of the pit too.

Henry and Dr. Snow hurried over to him.

York said, "The leaking cesspool contaminated the pump's water. I'll do a few more tests before I send you both a report." He waved to Henry and Dr. Snow.

"The mystery is solved," Henry said. "Dr. Snow, I owe you an apology. You were right. The disease was in the water."

"I don't need an apology," Dr. Snow said. "Please tell the leaders of your church about this. Tell everyone who will listen. Then maybe we can stop the next outbreak of cholera."

"I will," Henry said. "I will tell a lot of people. We now know how the disease spread. We can help people around here stay healthy."

Beth turned to Curate Whitehead. She asked, "Did you find the index case?"

"Yes. I found the first person to get sick," he said.

"Who was it?" Dr. Snow asked.

Henry sighed. "Mrs. Lewis's baby was the first to die. Mrs. Lewis probably washed the baby's diapers. Then she threw the water into the cesspool."

Beth pointed to the trench. "So the diaper

water leaked through the bricks into the well water," she said.

Henry nodded.

Dr. Snow said, "That makes logical sense."

Clyde gave a low whistle.

Rosie's brothers did the same.

Oscar barked.

Beth turned to Patrick. He looked sick to his stomach.

"Are you okay?" she asked.

"I drank water from this pump. And that dirty water has been leaking into the well. Yuck!" Patrick said. "I might get cholera."

"Wait. The Imagination Station can cure you," Beth whispered. "We just need to find the first liquid. Then it will reappear."

Patrick nodded.

Clyde said, "Soon we can put the handle back on the pump."

"Once the water is completely clean," Henry said. "That may take some time. But the handle's return will mark a good day."

"Did you know Mrs. Lewis's husband is sick now?" Patrick asked. "She'll clean his clothes and dump that water into the cesspool too."

"The leak from this cesspool will start the sickness again," Dr. Snow said. "Someone needs to report this cesspool. It must be repaired or removed. No one can drink the water. The pump handle needs to stay off for a while."

"I'll tell the board," Henry said. "They will take action."

"Very well. Goodbye, then," Dr. Snow said. He waved and left abruptly.

They all watched Dr. Snow hurry away.

"That's Dr. Snow's problem," Clyde said. "He is smart and dedicated. But his abrupt ways do not make him likable."

"Dr. Snow did figure things out," Henry said.

"But *you* will help everyone understand what caused the cholera outbreak," Patrick said.

"God put the right people in the right place at the right time," Beth said.

Cholera would stop spreading and people would stop dying, thanks to Dr. Snow. But the people in London would learn about it from Curate Whitehead.

Just then, Old Willie turned the corner onto Broad Street. "I've got you now!" he shouted. Two strong men were on either side of him.

14

Hiram's Store

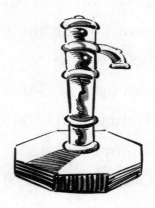

Patrick took a step behind the curate. He didn't want Old Willie to see him. He didn't want to go back to the workhouse.

Henry smiled. "How can I help you?" he asked Old Willie.

Old Willie stopped in front of him. His guards stopped on either side of him. "Give me back my worker," he said.

"Which one?" Henry asked.

"The one you took from me this morning," Old Willie said.

"I found many workers today," Henry said. He stepped aside and showed all five of the boys. They wore similar clothing and were all caked with dirt.

"I can't tell them apart," Old Willie said.

"That's fine," Henry said. "Tell me his name. Then I'll point him out to you."

"His name?" Old Willie said. "How would I know his name? I'm not his father."

"You can't tell me his name?" Henry asked. "Then I can't return the worker."

Old Willie's face turned red. "It's either that one or that one," he said. He pointed to Patrick and the youngest of Rosie's brothers.

"I doubt they'll tell you which is which," Henry said.

Old Willie leaned forward. His hands balled

into fists. "I know Clyde's name," he said. "He can return to the workhouse with me."

"That may be a problem," Henry said. "Clyde owns Hiram's Oil Store."

Old Willie gave a mean laugh. "Clyde won't be an owner of it for long. He has to pay rent tomorrow. But I hear he won't be able to do that. I'll be back for him in the morning," he said.

Oscar growled.

Old Willie backed up.

Oscar charged Old Willie with bared teeth. Old Willie and his guards fled.

Henry turned to Clyde. "I'm sorry, son. Come by the boardinghouse later. We'll figure out something," he said.

Henry held up Dr. Snow's map. "Dr. Snow forgot this. I must return it to him."

"Thank you for your help, Curate Whitehead," Patrick said.

"Helping people is what I do," Henry said.

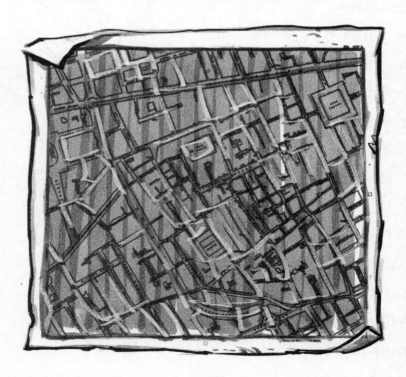

He gave each child a coin. Then he waved and walked down the street away from them.

The youngest of Rosie's brothers asked, "Should we fill in the hole?"

Clyde shook his head no. "York needs to do more testing," he said.

Rosie's brothers left. The youngest turned back to Patrick and Clyde. He said, "Thanks for stopping us from drinking that water." Then he hurried away with his brothers.

Patrick only wanted to do one thing. He wanted to search for the liquid for the Imagination Station. He had to find it. Only Whit's new invention inside the Imagination Station could cure him. But where could the liquid be?

Beth gave Patrick a smile. "Let's go to Hiram's Oil Store," she said.

"The store might have the liquid you need," Clyde said.

Beth said, "We can help you search for your uncle's will, too."

Clyde sighed. "One last time," he said.

Oscar trotted beside them to Hiram's Oil Store. He barked at the door.

"His bed is inside," Clyde said. "Oscar napped there every day. At night before my uncle closed the shop, he would pet Oscar. Then he and Oscar would head home."

Patrick scratched the top of Oscar's head.

Clyde took a key from his pocket. He unlocked the dark-green door. They all went inside the store.

Clyde lit an oil lamp. The light brightened the store.

Many types of oil were in glass jars on shelves. Some liquids were already in oil lamps.

Patrick liked the store. It smelled like something had just been painted.

Oscar hurried to a blanket in the far corner of the room. Then he sat on it.

Beth laughed. "That blanket isn't a throne," she said. "But you seem to like it." She started searching the store's shelves.

Patrick looked under the counter. "Your uncle had to put the money he made each day somewhere. What did your uncle do the same every night?" he asked.

"We dusted the shelves and put the oils

 away," Clyde said. He opened a cupboard. "We made a list of what was sold. Then my uncle petted and dethroned Oscar. I'd go in the back room to sleep."

"He dethroned Oscar?" Patrick asked. He walked toward Oscar. "What does that mean?"

"It meant Oscar had to leave his blanket," Clyde said. "So he could go home with my uncle."

Beth joined Patrick. "Maybe he meant something different," Beth said. She looked at Patrick.

Patrick nodded. "We need to dethrone Oscar," he said. He picked up the dog.

Beth pulled away the blanket. "Look," she said.

Clyde hurried over.

Under the blanket was a square board.

Patrick set Oscar down. He pulled up the board.

Below the floor was a dark metal box.

Patrick lifted it out of the hole. He said, "It has a keyless padlock on it."

"Those are new," Clyde said. "But I don't know the combination."

"Are there six numbers?" Beth asked.

Patrick nodded.

Beth was excited. She remembered the numbers on the ribbon. "Try 1-7-8-8-6-6," she said. She held her breath.

Clyde turned the dials and pulled.

Click! The padlock opened.

The Green Light

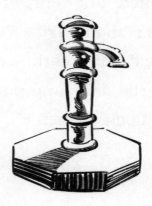

Patrick leaned forward.

Clyde opened the lid.

Inside was a stack of papers and coins. "Our rent money is here," Clyde said. He picked up the papers. "This is Uncle Hiram's will."

"Read it," Patrick said.

"I only know my numbers and letters for

customer names," Clyde said. He passed the paper to Patrick.

Patrick read it. He said, "Your uncle left everything to both your aunt and to you."

Clyde jumped up. "I have a way to make a living." Clyde laughed. "I have to tell my aunt," he said.

Patrick stood up. "This is great!" he said.

"But first," Clyde said, "let me help you." He went to the counter and put on a work apron. "Is this the liquid you're looking for?" he asked. He opened a jar.

Patrick and Beth smiled at each other.

Patrick took the black box out of his pocket. He placed its wand in the liquid. No green light. Clyde closed the lid and wiped the wand with an oil rag. He opened another jar.

Patrick put the wand in the oil. No green light.

Clyde opened container after container.

"Maybe the right liquid isn't here," Beth said.

Patrick was afraid Beth was right. But he was also scared about finding the right liquid. What if it didn't matter? What if the Imagination Station didn't return? What if they were stuck here for the rest of their lives?

Clyde went behind the counter. "Let's try the liquid from America," he said. He found the jar and opened it.

Patrick stuck the wand in the gray-blue liquid. The button on the box turned green.

"This is it!" Beth said.

Patrick whooped.

"How interesting," Clyde said. "I've never seen anything like that." Clyde turned the oil label around. "What does it say?"

Patrick said, "It's called Tesla's Oil."

Beth laughed. Tesla had helped Whit build the Model T Imagination Station. "Yay for Tesla's Oil!" she said.

"Wait," Patrick said. He leaned toward Beth and whispered, "This is 1854. Tesla wasn't born yet."

Beth whispered, "Maybe he kept trying to build a time machine. Maybe he sent this special oil back in time."

Patrick nodded. They might not know how the oil got to Hiram's Oil Store. But it was the oil they needed.

Patrick heard the hum of the Imagination Station. He smiled. The hum was a welcome sound. The Model T appeared outside the shop's large windows.

Patrick picked up the oil. "We have to go," Patrick said.

"Goodbye," Clyde said. "Thank you for all your help!"

Beth waved goodbye. "Thank you for yours, too," she said.

"You've saved my life," Patrick said.

"All I did was give you oil," Clyde said. He laughed.

Patrick followed Beth outside.

"I'm so glad to see the Imagination Station," Patrick said. "I thought we might be stuck here. I was afraid too much of its power source had leaked."

"Me too," Beth said. "But now we can go home."

Patrick hopped into the passenger seat.

Beth slid into the driver's seat.

Patrick found the compartment on the passenger side. He placed Tesla's oil inside.

Then he noticed a keyhole next to the compartment. He finally knew what his gift was for.

Patrick took the small key out of his pocket. It fit the lock perfectly. Patrick turned the key.

A sliding panel moved to cover the compartment. Then the panel opened. The container full of Tesla's oil was no longer there. The oil was now inside the Imagination Station.

Beth put on her seat belt. "Ready?" she asked.

Patrick left the key in the lock. He buckled his seat belt. He couldn't wait for the Imagination Station to cure him. He couldn't wait to go home.

Beth hit the big red button.

The Model T sprayed them with a fine mist.

"What's happening?" Beth asked.

Patrick laughed. "Maybe it found the cholera germ on me. No germs are leaving with us," he said. "That means I won't have cholera."

The Imagination Station made a loud squeak. Then metal scraped against metal.

"I must have been real sick," Patrick said. But something didn't feel right.

Patrick heard the sound of glass shattering. He looked at Beth.

"There's that smell again," Beth said.

Patrick smelled it too. There was the scent of apricots, lemons, pears, and oranges.

The fine mist grew into a heavier spray. Drops of water began to rain on the inside of the Model T.

Then everything went black.

Find out about the next adventure—*Swept into the Sea*— at TheImaginationStation.com.

Secret Word Puzzle

Patrick and Beth discovered the first liquid to keep the Imagination Station running. They also learned about cholera and overcame their fears. Now you can discover the cure for your fears.

Each number stands for a letter. Write the correct letter in each blank on the next page. The word in the boxes is the secret word.

1 W	5 H	9 N	13 T
2 D	6 A	10 Y	14 R
3 E	7 U	11 M	15 S
4 O	8 F	12 I	16 L

Secret Word Puzzle

$\overline{}_{1}$ $\overline{}_{5}$ $\overline{}_{3}$ $\overline{}_{9}$ $\qquad$ $\overline{}_{12}$ $\qquad$ $\overline{}_{6}$ $\overline{}_{11}$

$\overline{}_{6}$ $\overline{}_{8}$ $\overline{}_{14}$ $\overline{}_{6}$ $\overline{}_{12}$ $\overline{}_{2}$,

$\overline{}_{12}$ $\qquad$ $\overline{}_{1}$ $\overline{}_{12}$ $\overline{}_{16}$ $\overline{}_{16}$

☐ ☐ ☐ ☐ ☐ $\overline{}_{12}$ $\overline{}_{9}$
13 14 7 15 13

$\overline{}_{10}$ $\overline{}_{4}$ $\overline{}_{7}$

Go to **TheImaginationStation.com.**
Find the cover of this book.
Click on "Secret Word."
Type in the answer,
and you'll receive a prize.

About the Authors

AUTHOR CHRIS BRACK
loves to read all kinds of books, especially kids' books. She, her husband, and her sons share their house with Copper, a basset hound, and Ollie, a huge tomcat.

AUTHOR SHEILA SEIFERT
is an award-winning coauthor of many books, such as *Bible Kidventures: Stories of Danger and Courage*. She likes to find good books for kids to read. Parents can find her bimonthly book flyer at http://simpleliterature.com/bookclub/.

FOCUS ON THE FAMILY PRESENTS

THE IMAGINATION STATION

THE KEY TO ADVENTURE LIES WITHIN YOUR IMAGINATION.

1 VOYAGE WITH THE VIKINGS
2 ATTACK AT THE ARENA
3 PERIL IN THE PALACE
4 REVENGE OF THE RED KNIGHT
5 SHOWDOWN WITH THE SHEPHERD
6 PROBLEMS IN PLYMOUTH
7 SECRET OF THE PRINCE'S TOMB
8 BATTLE FOR CANNIBAL ISLAND
9 ESCAPE TO THE HIDING PLACE
10 CHALLENGE ON THE HILL OF FIRE
11 HUNT FOR THE DEVIL'S DRAGON
12 DANGER ON A SILENT NIGHT

13 THE REDCOATS ARE COMING!
14 CAPTURED ON THE HIGH SEAS
15 SURPRISE AT YORKTOWN
16 DOOMSDAY IN POMPEII
17 IN FEAR OF THE SPEAR
18 TROUBLE ON THE ORPHAN TRAIN
19 LIGHT IN THE LIONS' DEN
20 INFERNO IN TOKYO
21 MADMAN IN MANHATTAN
22 FREEDOM AT THE FALLS
23 TERROR IN THE TUNNEL
24 RESCUE ON THE RIVER
25 POISON AT THE PUMP

OVER 900,000 SOLD IN SERIES

COLLECT ALL OF THEM TODAY!

AVAILABLE AT A CHRISTIAN RETAILER NEAR YOU

WWW.TYNDALE.COM

CP0874